The Twelve Dancing Princesses

Activity Book and Play

Contents

Name: ___________________________

Class: ______   School: _______________

OXFORD
UNIVERSITY PRESS

Activities

Before you read, can you write the words?

~~soldier~~ castle king shoes notice

a

b

c

_____soldier_____ ________________ ________________

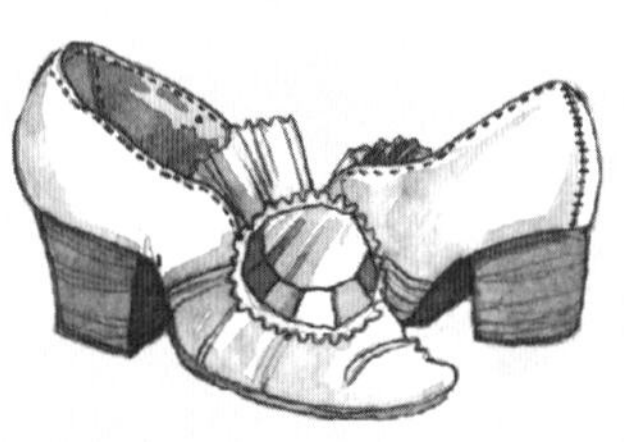

d

e

________________ ________________

1 The twelve princesses are daughters of the ______________ .

2 They all live in a ______________ .

3 Every morning the princesses are tired and have dirty

______________ .

4 The king can't understand it and writes a ______________ .

5 A ____soldier____ reads it and goes to the castle.

→ Pages 2–3

Circle the correct words. Then complete the sentences.

1 Once there was a king who had twelve ____*daughters*____ .

   sons   (daughters)   cats

2 Every night the king carefully ________________ the bedroom door.

   locked   opened   pushed

3 But every morning the princesses were ________________ .

   sad   afraid   tired

4 And their shoes were all dirty and full of ________________ .

   holes   food   water

5 The king could not ________________ it.

   understand   answer   hear

6 So he wrote ________________ .

   in a book   a notice   on the wall

7 'What do my daughters do every ________________ ?'

   morning   day   night

8 'Tell me – and you can ________________ one of them.'

   see   speak to   marry

9 A prince read the notice and came to the ________________ .

   castle   house   school

10 The king said, 'Watch my daughters ________________ .'

   quietly   carefully   softly

11 But the ________________ princess gave the prince a drink
and he went to sleep.

   oldest   youngest   nicest

12 In the morning he had ________________ to say to the king.

   something   anything   nothing

1 Write the words and number the sentences 1–5.

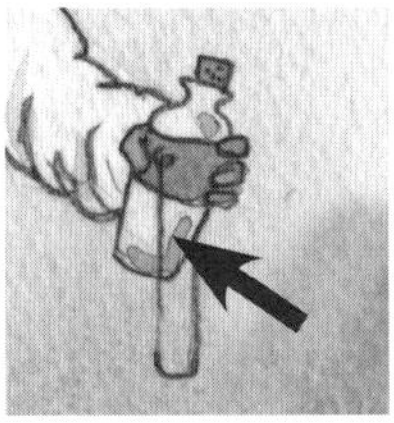

ctsale

castle

etiocn

____

tbotel

____

kolca

____

disoerl

____

a ☐ An old woman asked the ______________ to give her some water.

b ① Many princes came to the _____castle_____, but they saw nothing.

c ☐ The old woman gave him a magic ______________.

d ☐ Then one day a soldier came and read the ______________.

e ☐ He gave the old woman his ______________.

2 What does the old woman say? Complete the sentences using *will*, *must*, or *can*.

'The princesses _____will_____ give you a drink. But you ___________ not drink it. Do you hear me? You ___________ not go to sleep. You ___________ stay awake all night. Then you ___________ watch them.

'And look! You ___________ have this. It's a magic cloak. The princesses ___________ not see you when you wear this. You ___________ be invisible! Then you ___________ follow them.'

1 Answer the questions. Write *Yes* or *No*.

1 Are they in the castle? _____Yes_____
2 Did the soldier take the cup? __________
3 Did he drink from it? __________
4 Did he give the drink to the dog? __________
5 Are the soldier's eyes closed? __________
6 Is he asleep? __________
7 Is the dog asleep? __________

2 Complete the sentences with the past tense of these verbs.

> answer   see   sit   go   take   drink   put   open   ~~say~~
> follow   give   whisper   move

1 The oldest princess ___said___, 'Here, soldier! Have a nice drink!'
2 The soldier ______________ the cup.
3 He ______________ the drink to the dog.
4 The dog ______________ it and went to sleep.
5 Then the soldier ______________ down and closed his eyes.
6 'Is he asleep?' ______________ the youngest princess.
7 'Yes,' ______________ her sisters.
8 The princesses ______________ on their best dresses and their dancing shoes.
9 The oldest princess ______________ her bed.
10 Then she ______________ a door in the floor.
11 The soldier ______________ everything.
12 He put on his magic cloak and then he ______________ them.
13 They ______________ down the stairs.

→ Pages 8–9

1 Put the words in the correct order.

1 they the Down stairs went.

   Down the stairs they went.

2 The last princess youngest was.

   ____

3 was behind invisible her The soldier.

   ____

4 on Then dress her stepped he.

   ____

5 me someone There's behind!

   ____

6 following is Someone us!

   ____

2 Write the words.

soldier   quickly   silver   gold   princesses
fun   ~~strange~~   trees   beautiful   twelve

They came to a road of ___strange___ trees
all made of ______________ . The ______________
princesses walked ______________ . They looked
______________ and they were having so much
______________ .

Now they came to a road of trees all
made of ______________ . The ______________
danced through the ______________ and the
______________ watched them.

1 Answer the questions. Match the pictures with the sentences.

1 What were the trees made of?

☐ c *The trees were made of diamonds.*

2 What was there across the lake?

☐ ____________________________________

3 How many white boats were there on the water?

☐ ____________________________________

4 Who danced with the twelve princes?

☐ ____________________________________

2 Circle the mistake in each sentence. Then write the correct word.

1 The princesses were happy because they could see the (sky).

____*lake*____

2 In every boat a prince was talking. ____________

3 The soldier jumped into the boat with the youngest princess.

____

4 Her prince said, 'It feels empty.' ____________

5 The twelve princesses danced with the twelve kings. ____________

6 At last the ground began to grow light. ____________

7 The oldest princess cried, 'It will soon be night, sisters!'

____

➡ Pages 12–13

1 Make sentences about the story. Then write them in the correct order.

But the soldier ran faster and …	went to bed.
The twelve princesses and the twelve princes	got to the bedroom first.
The princesses ran through the trees and back …	across the lake.
The princesses saw him on the chair and …	up the stairs.
The princes rowed the princesses back …	ran out of the castle.

1 *The twelve princesses and the twelve princes ran out of the castle.*

2 ____

3 ____

4 ____

5 ____

2 What does the king say? Write the words.

same   ~~shoes~~   midday   holes   girls   dirty   asleep

'Look at these ____shoes____ ! They are all ____________ and full of ____________ . It's the ____________ every day. And look at these ____________ ! They are still ____________ and it's nearly ____________ !'

→ Pages 14–15

Write the words. Then complete the sentences.

1 t l o d e s *oldest*
2 l f o r o _______
3 e w a k a _______
4 w i t s g _______
5 e o o l f d l w _______
6 t o e u g y n s _______

7 l k a e _______
8 v i n l i s e b i _______
9 e d i o l s r _______
10 y h e v a _______
11 s i a r t s _______
12 c a g i m _______

a That night the _______ followed the princesses again.
b He gave his drink to his dog and he stayed _______ .
c The soldier put on his _______ cloak.
d He became _______ .
e The _______*oldest*_______ daughter moved back her bed.
f She opened a door in the _______ .
g All the princesses went down the _______ .
h The soldier _______ them.
i He took _______ from the trees.
j At the _______ , there were the twelve white boats and the twelve princes.
k The soldier got into the boat with the _______ princess.
l Her prince said, 'The boat feels _______ again tonight.'

1 Choose a, b, or c.

1 At the castle the princesses and the princes had a ... time.
  a ☐ strange   b ☐ sad   c ☑ wonderful

2 Then the twelve princesses ran back to the ...
  a ☐ lake   b ☐ castle   c ☐ sea

3 The princes rowed them back ... the water.
  a ☐ through   b ☐ across   c ☐ around

4 The soldier ran up the stairs ... the princesses.
  a ☐ above   b ☐ before   c ☐ behind

5 The soldier got to the room ...
  a ☐ first   b ☐ second   c ☐ last

6 The king asked the soldier, 'Did you see ... ?'
  a ☐ anyone   b ☐ everything   c ☐ anything

2 Complete the sentences with the past tense of these verbs.

run ~~dance~~ whisper begin call say think come get sit

1 At the castle the princesses ____danced____ with their princes.
2 The soldier _____________ , 'How beautiful this is!'
3 At last the sky _____________ to grow light.
4 The oldest princess _____________ , 'It's time to go home to bed!'
5 The princesses and the princes _____________ back to the lake.
6 The soldier _____________ to the room first.
7 He _____________ on the chair and closed his eyes.
8 The oldest princess _____________ , 'He's asleep!'
9 Later that morning the king _____________ .
10 The soldier _____________ , 'Give me one more night.'

1 Circle the correct words. Then write sentences.

1 What did the soldier put on?

a silver hat   some gold trousers   (his magic cloak)

The soldier put on his magic cloak.

2 At the castle, what did he take?

a big diamond   a beautiful glass cup   a silver twig

____

3 Where did he put it?

in his pocket   in a bag   on the floor

____

4 What did the soldier tell the king?

something   everything   nothing

____

2 Write the words.

1 

a ... cup

2 The trees were made of silver, ...,
and diamonds.

3 not sleeping

4 when something really happens

5 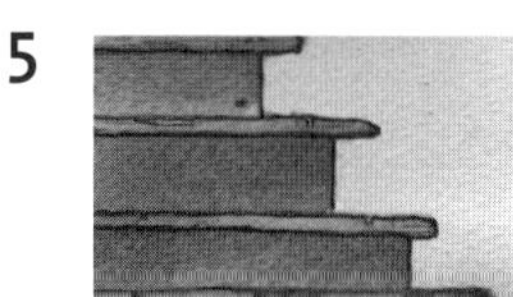

6 The soldier ... the oldest princess.

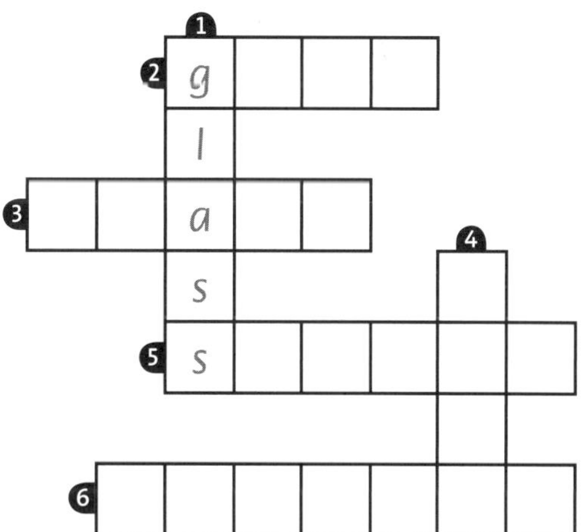

 Play 

Act the play.

Characters

 Chorus

 King

 Oldest princess

 Youngest princess

 Princesses (10)

 Prince 1
(no words to speak)

 Soldier

 Old woman

 Prince 2

 Princes (11)
(no words to speak)

 Pages 2–3    *Scene 1*

Chorus: Once there was a king who had twelve daughters. Every morning the princesses were tired. And their shoes were all dirty and full of holes. The king could not understand it. He wrote a notice: 'What do my daughters do every night? Tell me – and you can marry one of them and be king one day.'

 Scene 2

Chorus: A prince read the notice and came to the castle. But the oldest princess gave him a drink and he went to sleep. So he saw nothing.

Scene 3

Chorus: Then one day a soldier came and read the notice.

Old woman: Can you give me some water?

Soldier: Here you are! … I am going to the castle.

Old woman: Thank you. Listen. Those princesses will give you a drink. You must not drink it. You must stay awake. Have this magic cloak. You will be invisible!

Scene 4

Oldest princess: Here, soldier! Have a nice drink!

Chorus: The soldier took the cup. But he did not drink. He sat down and closed his eyes.

Youngest princess (*quietly*): Is he asleep?

Princesses: Yes! Come on! Let's have some fun!

Chorus: The princesses put on their best dresses and their dancing shoes.

Oldest princess: Come on! Let's go!

Chorus: The oldest princess opened a door in the floor. Quickly the soldier put on his magic cloak. Then he followed them.

➡ Pages 8–11

🍃 Scene 5 🍃

Chorus: The youngest princess was last. The invisible soldier was behind her. He stepped on her dress.

Youngest princess: Who's there? There's someone behind me.

Princesses: We can't see anyone!

🍃 Scene 6 🍃

Chorus: The princesses came through some strange trees all made of silver, gold, and diamonds. Then they could see the lake. Across the lake there was a wonderful castle. There were twelve boats on the water. In every boat a prince was waiting. The soldier stepped into the boat with the youngest princess.

Prince 2: This boat feels different tonight. It feels heavy.

Youngest princess: Perhaps the weather is too warm for you.

🍃 Scene 7 🍃

Chorus: At the castle, the twelve princesses danced with the twelve princes. The soldier watched them. At last the sky began to grow light.

Oldest princess: It will soon be day, sisters! It's time to go home to bed!

→ Pages 12–15

 Scene 8

Chorus: The princesses and the princes ran out of the castle. The princes rowed the princesses back across the lake. Then the princesses ran back to their bedroom. But the soldier ran faster. He got to the room first.

Oldest princess: Look! He's asleep. To bed, sisters ... to bed!

 Scene 9

Chorus: Later that morning the king came.

King: Look at these shoes! They are all dirty and full of holes. And look at these girls! They are still asleep. Did you see anything?

Soldier: Yes, I did. But I need to see more. Let me watch again tonight.

King: OK! Good luck!

Scene 10

Chorus: That night the soldier followed the princesses again. It was the same as the night before. The princesses ran through the trees. The soldier took a little silver twig. *Crack!* Then he took a little gold twig. *Crack!* And a little diamond twig. *Crack!*

Youngest princess: What was that noise? Is someone following us?

Princesses: We can't see anyone! Come on!

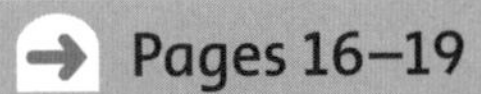 Scene 11 

Chorus: At the castle, the princesses danced with their princes. At last the sky began to grow light. The princesses ran back. But the soldier was faster.

Scene 12

Chorus: Later that morning the king came.

King: Did you see anything?

Soldier: Yes, I did. But give me one more night.

Scene 13

Chorus: That night the soldier followed the princesses again. At the castle he took one of the glass cups.

Scene 14

Chorus: In the morning the soldier told the king everything. He gave him the twigs and the glass cup.

King *(to the princesses)*: Is this true?

Princesses: Yes, Father.

King: Well, soldier ... which one do you want to marry?

Soldier: I think your oldest daughter is the one for me.

Scene 15

Chorus: The soldier married the oldest princess and they were very happy.

The End